TRY NOT TO DIE

In a

Hell Hole

a short story

by

JOHN PALISANO

Download Your Free Copy

Includes the first 2 chapters and 1 death scene from each of the first 7 books in the Try Not to Die series.

Try Not to Die

In A Hell Hole

Nasty water is spreading out from under the bathroom door. "This place is a real hell hole." I lock eyes with Emma, my co-worker at Infinity Storage in lovely San Enare, California. "I swear to God, it's always something with this place." I shrug. "Good thing I like hell holes."

Emma shakes her head. "Fix one thing, someone breaks something else." She smiles. "It's better than having no job. We know what that's like, Blair, don't we?"

"Yup. Just tired of the parade of freaks in here doing stuff like this."

"I don't even remember anyone coming in here tonight," Emma says, "which means no one's asked me for the bathroom key."

"Same," I say. "Must've been someone from the day shift. Either that or Nicky gave it to someone."

Emma laughs. "I've heard of hole-in-the-wall bars, but we're a hole-in-the-ground extra storage place."

"You mean hole-in-the-wall storage place?" I cock my head.

Emma turns away. "Yeah. Right. Whatever." She sways. Puts out her arms like she's about to fall. The entire place moves. Rumbles.

I put my hands out, too. "Quake." My thoughts race. What are we supposed to do? There isn't a desk to hide under. All the doors are shut with heavy doors. There's nowhere to hide.

"It's a big one." Emma sounds cool and detached like she's in shock.

"What do we do?" I ask, more from instinct than believing she has any idea.

"Wait it out," Emma says.

More violent, the shaking makes me crouch just to stay upright. "Holy shit."

Loud bangs jar us. The row of handcarts fall over, their metal banging onto the hard tile flooring.

The floor rolls back and forth like we're in a carnival funhouse. Emma stares between her feet, her arms still outstretched in a surfing pose. "It's like it's right under us," she says, her voice so high.

An insanely loud bang makes us look out past the lobby toward the main staging room. Something large fills the area.

"Is that the ceiling?" I can't believe what I'm seeing. "The AC unit?"

The shaking stops. The rumbling cuts out.

"Is that it?" I ask.

Emma opens her mouth to speak, but a violent jolt knocks us.

I can't feel my feet. Looking down, I see I'm a few feet up off the ground.

It's as though we're cats on a bed and someone just flipped the blanket to shake us off.

We're both several feet in the air, Emma hunched over like a wolf. "Blair!" Her voice sounds drawn out like it's in slow motion.

A sound like a million tons of metal crashes around us. I'm going to die. Right now. I'm sure my heart stops. This is it. The end.

My feet smash into the buckled floor. The impact sends shard-like sensations through my heels up into my hips. I clench my jaw.

As much as I try, I can't find my balance and topple backward. I curl at my elbows and roll onto my side. I gasp, winded by the impact.

The shaking subsides, but I stay down, trying to calm my breathing.

"Emma?" I look around but see no trace of my friend. "You here?" I wonder if Emma's found something to duck underneath. Maybe she's forgotten something?

I sit up and look with more intention. Call out again.

With each passing second, I feel increasingly sure she took off running or is dead.

Where'd she go so fast?

Past the main receiving room, beyond the fallen ceiling and AC unit, is the wide open main door leading into the storage units. Smoke billows out. I stand and step out from behind the desk area.

The floor of the front lobby is broken and buckled in a hundred places. Concrete and rebar poke out from the cracked tile pieces. Is the foundation of the building sound? This whole place could come down if it isn't. Infinity Storage isn't a chain with brand-new construction. They've been in business for decades, so there are a lot of things that need tending on their best day, let alone after a massive quake.

I edge my way out from behind the desk and front lobby and stand in the doorway leading toward the main area. Everything's trashed. The AC broke the floor. Tile litters the area. Two lines stretch down from the ceiling and end inside the unit. Still plugged into power. Probably the other cable is a drainage pipe. Stay the heck away from it. This isn't a job worth dying for. Not even close to it.

I cup my hands around my mouth. "Emma! Nicky!" I hear nothing back.

The place rumbles and shakes. Just a bit. "Aftershock," I say, recalling sometimes the second or even the seventh aftershocks might be equally as powerful as the initial jolt. I need to get out.

Navigating the huge buckles in the floor, I make my way around the hulking AC unit and head for the front door. The wire stretching down from the ceiling might be live and could electrocute me. Hell. Maybe the ground's already buzzing with lethal voltage.

I stop. Maybe this is a stupid idea. I should wait for someone to come.

But I know better. No one's coming. I'd have to call them. Even then? By the time they got here, what would they do? I can probably find a safe place out by then, anyway. Got to be your own damn advocate.

It doesn't take long to see a huge metal flange from the back of the AC unit has fallen right up against the doors, blocking them. And the windows are a no-go, double-paned on each side and metal titanium mesh within the glass. They were designed to thwart smash-and-grabbers, after all. "I'm trapped."

I smell water, like the kind when you go hiking or camping. Outside water. Not the stuff from the tap. There's something mixed with it, too, like spoiled fruit.

Turning left, I consider going into the depths of the storage facility. Emma must have hurried off down there. Where else could she have gone? There is nowhere else to go.

***

The hallways appear endless. Without the running lights, they seem to stretch into nothingness. My throat tightens. I don't want to be doing this. It'd be better if I stayed the hell out of here. Doesn't feel right.

My boots thud as I cross the concrete floors. "Emma? Where are you?" My stomach feels super tight. I wonder if there's a way out from inside the storage halls.

Yup. Emergency exits flank on either side of the building. Management has a strict policy against using them. Well, this earthquake shit totally counts as an emergency. I'm not staying here just because they say so. I'm out. They can keep their stupid damn job if they want to fire me over it. What do I have to lose? Mom and Dad passed away when I was a kid. Been living by myself for years. I'll be fine. Always land on my feet.

Just have to get to an exit. Dim emergency lights glow along the top of the hall. The tiny LEDs do little more than mark a path. I can't see far. Twenty feet in front, smoke blocks the way. Can't tell if it's from dust or fire. Everything smells like plaster, drywall, and … burning. Crap. Hope this place isn't on fire. Hope it's not in front of me. Putting out a hand, the air feels cooler instead of warmer.

"That's weird." Maybe it has something to do with the downed AC unit; maybe the fluid escaped and flash-froze.

Something bangs against the metal door inside a unit nearby and scares the shit out of me; my heart's firmly in my throat.

"What the…?"

Another bang, louder than the first, rings out across the hallway, echoing down its length.

Something moans. Growls. Something big's inside the storage unit.

I want to run back to the front but those doors are blocked. No choice but to run forward to get past whatever's inside the unit making the noise and get to the other side of the facility to the emergency doors.

My heart feels made from lead. My throat goes dry. No time like now. I race ahead as more bangs come from the units to my right. It's as though whatever was in the first unit's also smashing all the units.

The sound follows. So loud, like a hammer with a cinder block head, smashing against the inner walls. Get me out of here. This is insane. Supposed to be people's stuff inside the storage units.

Wonder why or what was inside them making such a racket. Did Emma dose me? Maybe this is all a hallucination? Maybe this is all in my mind and there aren't really noises. Maybe it's not monsters or creatures at all, but some reasonable explanation.

The smoke's so thick at the end of the first hallway, I can't spot anything that'd make a good landmark to be able to find my way out. If I keep going there's a good chance

I'm gonna get lost. And if the whole place goes up in flames, I'm dead.

The horrible banging sounds subsided. That's because they can't smell me.

I should know better than to entertain such an idea—that there's actually some kind of living being inside the facility, chasing me on the other side of the storage unit doors, crashing through brick and steel walls. Can't be real, whatever this is.

It's probably the plumbing going or the lines that bring in the electricity or the gas lines. Oh god if it's the gas lines, and they were making those huge knocking noises. This place is probably filled with odorless gas right now. And the slightest spark is going to light it up. Crap. I better get the hell out of here and fast Where, though?

"Hey."

I jump, spin around, and see Nicky and her nervous smile.

"What is that?" she asks. "Where's Emma?"

"I don't know, but we have to go," I say, a bit out of breath.

"Yeah," Nicky says. "Follow me."

The sound. Louder.

Nicky's gray-blonde ponytail bounces as she hurries away and down the hall. There's no guarantee she knows where she's going and part of me thinks the hallway to the right is a better choice.

What will you do?

Follow Nicky. Go to page 10.
Go your own way. Go to page 8.

Nicky's always been like another family member to me. Half older sister, half-mom, she's been the rare human being that actually is more human than just being. She's never led me wrong. "Come on," she says. "We can take the emergency exits out at the end of the hall."

"Okay," I say, trusting her. Makes sense, after all.

The banging comes back, this time right in front of us as the hall makes a sharp right. The thing is inside one of the units.

"Nicky?" I call out. "You sure this is right?"

"I don't ... know," she says.

I don't like the hesitancy in her voice and stop walking. In fact, I step back. My stomach goes tight. Something just ain't right.

Boom!

Everything shakes. Lifts. It's like being on a big slide. I grab onto a huge support pole, wrapping myself around it as tight as possible. The storage doors open and everything inside slides away from us. Doesn't compute at first, but mattresses and boxes and brooms appear to be sucked into a black hole. I can feel the pressure of the air all around me.

But it's not a black hole like from space. It's in the here and now.

And I can't hold on much longer.

Infinity Storage tilts more. Nicky's holding onto the side of the unit by one small metal pole. She looks up at me, her face wide and afraid. I go to say something, but before I can, a side table smashes into her head. She loses her grip and drops into the darkness beyond.

Something hits me from behind and I see stars, my grip loosening. No. Hold on. But my body is divorced from my mind. It's like I'm watching things unfold from deep inside myself, unable to do anything about it.

I fall toward the hole where the storage unit had been. Only bits of its walls remain.

Sliding right past in a blink, cold air hits me. For a moment, it feels like I'm flying.

A soft blue light rushes up toward me, or I toward it.

My feet hit first, my legs losing feeling as they dissolve in the blue hot lava. There's not even enough time for pain as I sink. Just a white flash.

You should have followed Nicky. Go to page 10.

My gut tells me not to go headfirst down the hall. The shaking seems to be coming from. "Nicky?" I call out, thinking I might persuade her back.

No answer.

She's long gone, into the smoke.

Boom!

The things behind the walls hit again. And again.

I'm not going forward, so the only way I can go is left, down another long hall of storage units. There's less smoke. Nothing banging inside the storage units as far as I can tell. Yet. My lungs feel like I've inhaled a hundred cigars or stood over a campfire all night. My head hurts. My nose feels stopped up. Breathing is not going so well.

Something looks different ahead. The halls are long, but no more than a few hundred feet. There's a blue glow. I slow down and walk carefully. Take a moment to look behind and over my shoulder.

The blue light gets brighter with each step I take. The edges of the hall look torn and tattered like something's ripped right through it. Earthquake. Got to be an earthquake.

What about the rumblings? Likely water pipes or something. Everything is damaged. God only knows what's broken and waiting behind the storage unit doors.

The place tilts. I go to grab onto something, but there's nothing to latch onto. I bend down to keep my balance and notice the entire hall angled down a bit more. I have no choice but to step closer. Cold air blows over me, the likes of which I haven't felt in ages. Not sure how that's even possible. Maybe there'll be a crack somewhere and I can wiggle my way out of the building.

At the edge of the hall, I can tell the blue light is coming from below. There are pieces of rebar sticking out from broken concrete, so I grab one to steady myself and look over and down.

There's a body, slumped. Impaled on three pieces of rebar like a barbecue chicken skewer. Emma. Face down. She probably made it until everything tilted, too. Damn it. I cross myself out of habit.

A hole in the ground stretches for what I'd guess is a few hundred feet around. It goes down farther than I can tell. Below is a pool of the same kind of blue I'd seen above. The blue flows like some kind of underground lake. Or a river. Yeah. River. It's definitely moving.

What the hell?

The fluid glows the same uncanny blue. Chills run through me. Is this toxic waste or something? Why's it so cold? How'd this hole happen?

Maybe it's a sinkhole, opened up from the tremors. That'd make sense. The liquid's got to be some kind of corporate dumping, I bet. Shoot. That's got to be something really deadly to be glowing bright blue. Probably nuclear.

Ah, crap. If it's nuclear runoff, I'm a goner. No doubt. Already too late. Like the first responders at Chernobyl, I'll have radiation poisoning in no time, at the very least. If the radiation itself doesn't just strike me down within the hour.

Stop. Don't think like that. You don't know that.

I do, though. You can't smell or feel radiation, can you? And it'd make sense it's cold because they'd need to keep it cold.

But there ain't a nuclear plant anywhere out here or anywhere close. Not that I'm aware of. That doesn't mean they couldn't have been dumping this stuff under our feet for decades without telling any of us.

More reason for me to get out as soon as possible. Stop staring at the stuff and just get the hell out.

I climb down and off the edge of the broken hallway onto a small outcropping of rock. There's lots of stuff to grab and hold onto. The foundation's exposed and there's rubble. I make it about ten feet down and off the hallway and look back up. I half expect Nicky to pop out, but she doesn't. "Adios," I say and continue down.

There's a small ledge that appears it'll give me a sightline on finding a way out. I climb down onto it, grateful for the blue light as it illuminates everything just enough to see all the details.

Everything shakes and I grab hold of a small outcropping of rock to keep my balance and not fall off the small ledge.

A loud noise startles me from behind—like a million tons of rocks falling. Not too far off, I see the entire path I'd walked down tumble into the blue lava river. *Shit. Shit. Shit.*

The rumble stops. But now what?

A big portion of the building's bottom hovers over the open hole. The earth just opened up underneath, somehow. My bet's the underground toxic river finally carved enough away to make it all unstable. Just my luck, it happens during my shift.

Worry about that later. Just leave. Now. Focus.

The blue river seems closer. More so than it should be given how far down I've climbed. As I watch, it's obvious it's rising. Not a whole lot, but enough.

Try Not to Die: In a Hell Hole

I scramble down one ledge, some of the bluc lava's already boiling over the bottom. To my left there's another ledge. I recognize some of those pieces on there as being our carts—the hand dollies and push carts tenants use to move their stuff in and out. They've all fallen from the end of the storage area and are bunched up. They're made of metal. It'll take them a bit to melt. Not impervious but much better than plastic.

My throat feels on fire, my eyes tight and dry, like there's a rim of crust around their edges. The gas from the lava is overwhelming and my head is aching. This stuff must be toxic. Probably will kill me. Probably take out anyone else exposed to it for too long.

I check my pants pocket and pull out the stupid mask we had to wear during the pandemic. It's gone through the wash but it's one of the good cloth ones Mom made for me. Even so, I hate them. But damn I'm glad I have it. Covering my nose and mouth takes just a moment but I immediately feel better. Instead of the harsh, burning metal smell, it's the dollar store fabric softener I use. Is it working? I don't know, long term. Not like it's a gas mask. But maybe it'll give me a fighting chance. Just enough to maybe get the heck out of this hell hole.

The world shakes again as I scurry down the small ledge and toward the carts. Something huge falls right in front of me and into the lava.

It's eaten up in a split second. There's a bubble. Which rises. Pops.

Lava sprays upward. I race toward the carts and fall on my butt, sliding with my right leg in front of me like I'm stealing first base. It hurts but I'm able to reach out and grab the sides of a cart and lift it upward. I crouch underneath, careful to take my hands off the sides.

Lava spray sizzles on top of the cart. Some of it lands in little drops around me, scalding the rock instantly.

My heart skips. Did I get burned at all? Any on me?

I calm down, realizing I'm safe. For now.

Then I spot it. A purple sneaker, jammed near the other carts. Nikki's. But there's no sign of her. I look at it longer and see a rim of glistening red around the foot hole. My guts tighten. She's gone.

I inch out from under the cart and look. The hallway from the storage place is high above and too far back. Inaccessible. Crap. If only I'd waited in the lobby. What was I thinking?

But no. Had I stayed inside, who knows what would still be standing? What if the entire place collapsed? All that stuff on top of me? I'd be a mound of jelly in a split instant.

I made the right choice. The only choice.

Just don't second-guess yourself. You're here now. Focus. Figure it out.

The carts. Right. Use them.

On the back of my cart, there's a large push handle. I grab it and slide it to the side. There are two more push carts and three hand dollies, and a space about twenty feet between the end of my ledge and the underside of the underground sinkhole. It leads up and out into the night sky.

Lucky or unlucky, the blue lava has risen high, quickly. It's no longer hundreds of feet down to its flow—it's maybe a dozen. If I don't try something it's going to rise and consume me, regardless. Do or die.

I stand, step toward a hand dolly and take it. I drop it onto the lava with the idea it'll act as a buffer that I can then toss a push dolly on top of before they both melt.

No such thing can happen because the hand dolly vanishes in seconds. Sinks right into the lava, heating up and glowing yellow and gold within seconds. I'd have no time. The plan won't work.

Crap. Crap. Crap.

The smell of the lava gets worse. It's cold. And it's rising. If I don't figure something out soon, I'm toast.

I am not going to die today, damn it.

Something stirs inside the lava. A dome-shaped bubble rises. Pops. A glistening coil unravels, reminding me so much of a sleeping millipede.

The coil's middle lifts and a pineapple-shaped end unravels rows of spikes as long as my forearm.

I've got a worse problem on my hands than the blue lava.

Stretching upward like a cobra, the uncoiled arm—if that's what it is—reaches way over my head. If only I could jump on and ride it like Jack and the Beanstalk or Paul Atreides and a sand worm. It's glistening with blue lava, though, and I'd be sure to be scalded. Plus, it'd sense me and shake me off. Neither good outcomes.

As the appendage travels upward, the lava goes down. Way down. Fast. Like how a tide goes out when there's a tsunami coming.

Which means exactly what?

Several stories down below, the appendage connects to a larger body. Of course it does, the part sticking up is its tail. I go cold realizing that the tail is likely what I heard crashing through the insides of the units, trying to find a way out. Now that it has ... what will it do?

The thing rises from the lava, going higher and higher, towering over my head in seconds. What the hell is this creature? Lord only knows.

Everything shakes as it rises up, too. It's glistening, coated in whatever the blue lava is. Better not get any of it on me—not even a drop.

The beast keeps rising. Following its tail is a shiny, leathery flap. Its armature of bones stretches outward, a triple claw at its end, with one nail chipped and raw. The dark wing spreads upward and then, when it clears the top of the sinkhole, spreads outward at least 200 feet. It's followed by a second wing.

It's crawling backward up and out of the hole.

A curled claw ascends, its muscles strong and fat like those of a dragon. But this is not a dragon. This is a hell beast. Its scales aren't red or gold or ornamental; they're dark as pitch. Blue flames linger in spots.

I cower behind my makeshift shield. How the heck am I going to escape? There's nowhere to run. It's going to see any small gesture, for sure. I can't even be sure the damn cart is really covering me fully. Anything with half a brain ...

Its eye flares at me. I can sense it before I see it. Behind me, the creature stares. I can see a blurry reflection on the cart's metal surface. It's found me out.

A sound gathers. Its pitch is low and steady, but soon snowballs into a deafening roar.

The sound is unbelievable and I have to let go of the cart to cover my ears. The pressure on my ears and head feels a thousand times worse than being on a jet and having your ears pop.

It smells like a thousand pounds of sea life burnt to ash. I can taste it all the way down my throat. I'm about to gag when an immense claw the size of a tree trunk wraps around my middle.

I'm lifted and off the ledge, high into the sky in seconds. My stomach clenches. I'm going to die. This is how a mouse feels in the claws of an owl before it's torn in two.

Our town is a beautiful ruin. Orange fires rage from several tears in the earth. Buildings blaze. Many have fallen to rubble. There is no electric light anywhere. No car lights. No signs of life.

Something inside me lights up.

I like it.

This is a dream. Yes. A secret wish I've harbored. I'm happy seeing the world brought down. The apocalypse, if that's what this is, is pretty appealing. No work. No having to pretend to be nice. Lots of alone time. Maybe a lot of people were taken out. I know. Harsh of me. Uncaring. But being in the creature's grasp seems to have woken these sleeping desires.

There is something stuck in my side. A tickling feeling that hurts like a needle. It's inside me. Like a mosquito's proboscis. Is this why my thoughts have gone to such forbidden fantasies? Has the beast infused me with its hatred for humanity? Only now my feelings can be free just as it's been freed from its underground prison.

We fly downward and the beast places me on the ground with a precision and gentleness I'm not expecting.

It unwraps its claw and its proboscis slips out from my side. I don't want it out. I want it out. Need both.

The beast leans down, its face not like that of a human, but more insect-like. Its rows of eyes blink and I feel a dark flash inside my head. For a moment all seems inverted. Somehow, I can see farther across the wastelands. It is like some otherworldly night vision. And in places I can see something else in the dark scape. They're faint, but the auras of living things cling and crawl about. And as my focus sharpens, I see more in the auras. I see their blood. Their heart. Their minds.

My whole body is hungry, starved to find them, and drain them of their essence and store it inside me at my middle. A new pouch has grown inside me, a new organ where their juice will go. I know this instinctively. And know, too, that when I'm filled, the pressure will become unbearable. The hell beast Athka will come and tear into me. The relief will be short lived as I will succumb to the harvesting, but I will not die tonight. No. Tonight I will begin the hunt to stay alive.

Above me, Athka vanishes into the moonlit sky and I know what I've become. I wear the devil's smile and wonder if the world will ever again see the sun rise.

The end.

A Note to the Reader

I sure hope you enjoyed reading *Try Not to Die In A Hell Hole*. It was inspired by a recent move and my renting a storage unit. One afternoon, the entire place shook. Was it a semi passing by? A small tremor? Not sure, but that fear sparked my imagination. What if it was something much more sinister? And who knows: maybe we'll see more about what happened in San Enare, California down the road.

If you enjoyed this story, I bet you'll love *Try Not to Die In the Pandemic* and *Try Not to Die: In the Wild West* both of which I co-authored with Mark Tullius. Scroll down to check out more of my work and the *Try Not to Die* series. As independent creators, reviews on your preferred platforms make a profound difference, so please consider taking a moment and sharing your honest thoughts.

Out Now from John Palisano

NOVELS
"Night of 1,000 Beasts"
"Dust of the Dead"
Coming Soon in a new edition!
"Ghost Heart"
Now in a new paperback edition!
"Nerves"

NOVELLAS
"Placerita" with Lisa Morton
Coming December 2023 from Cemetery Dance
"Glass House"
"The Bipolar Express"
in Surreal Worlds

COLLECTIONS
"Starlight Drive—Four Tales for Halloween"
from Western Legends
"All That Withers—Stories"
*Collected Short Fiction
from Cytraxis Press*

DON'T STOP TRYING NOT TO DIE

Out Now

Try Not to Die: At Grandma's House
It's Grandma's house – quiet, cozy, nestled on a little mountain in West Virginia. What could possibly go wrong? A lot. So watch your back. Choose wisely. One misstep will get you and your little sister killed.

Try Not to Die: In Brightside
Mark and 10th Planet Jiu Jitsu teammate Dawna Gonzales continue the Brightside saga, bridging the gap between the first book and sequel, this time from the eyes of a female teenage telepath.

Try Not to Die: In the Pandemic
Mark and John Palisano take readers on the most intense hour they will ever spend on a cruise ship in this non-stop interactive adventure.

Try Not to Die: In the Wizard's Tower
Your name is Lucky. Your entire life you have lived at the Inn at the base of the impenetrable Wizard's Tower. But now you're stuck inside the mysterious Tower, mercy to its puzzles, traps, creatures...and magic.

Try Not to Die: In the Wild West
Mark and John Palisano return with a wild ride through the Old West. 30 ways to die on this little trip to Placerita Town.

Try Not to Die: At Ghostland
Duncan Ralston honored Mark by allowing the TNTD series to enter his incredible Ghostland world. This is the most brutal of all the books to date.

Try Not to Die: At Dethfest
Mark and Glenn Hedden bring TNTD to the Midwest and the coolest heavy metal concert to date.

Try Not to Die: Back at Grandma's House
Nice job escaping Grandma's house. Now you better get your ass back there if you want to save your family.

Coming Soon

Try Not to Die: At Summer Camp
Mark and Caitlin Marceau explore the Canadian wilderness.

Try Not to Die: In a Dark Fairy Tale
Mark and Evan Baughfman take a pair of princes on a death-filled adventure.

Plus 15 others in the works.

About the Author

John Palisano's novels include *Dust of the Dead, Ghost Heart, Nerves*, and *Night of 1,000 Beasts*. His novellas include *Glass House* and *Starlight Drive: Four Halloween Tales*. His first short fiction collection *All that Withers* celebrates over a decade of short story highlights.

He won the Bram Stoker Award© in short fiction for "Happy Joe's Rest Stop" and Colorado's Yog Soggoth award in 2018. More short stories have appeared in anthologies from Weird Tales, Cemetery Dance, PS Publishing, Independent Legions, Space & Time, Dim Shores, DarkFuse, Crystal Lake, Terror Tales, Lovecraft eZine, Horror Library, Bizarro Pulp, Written Backwards, Dark Continents, Big Time Books, McFarland Press, Darkscribe, Dark House, Omnium Gatherum, and more.

Non-fiction pieces have appeared in Blumhouse Online, Fangoria, and Dark Discoveries magazines and he's been quoted in Vanity Fair, The Writer, and the Los Angeles Times.

You can find more at: www.johnpalisano.com

Published by Vincere Press
65 Pine Ave., Ste 806
Long Beach, CA 90802

Try Not to Die: In a Hell Hole
Copyright © 2023 by John Palisano

All rights reserved.
For information about permission to reproduce selections from this book, write to Permissions, Vincere Press, 65 Pine Avenue Ste. 806, Long Beach, CA 90802

This is a work of fiction. All of the characters and events portrayed in this book are either fictitious or used fictitiously. Any resemblance to actual persons, living or dead, events or locales is entirely coincidental.

Printed in the United States of America
First Edition

ISBN: 978-1-961740044

Front cover by Jun Ares

Made in the USA
Middletown, DE
01 October 2023